We Three Kings from
Pepper Street Prime

Also in the Redwing Series

Joan Smith

We Three Kings from Pepper Street Prime

Illustrated by Nicole Goodwin

Julia MacRae Books
A division of Franklin Watts

Text © 1985 Joan Smith
Illustrations © 1985 Nicole Goodwin
All rights reserved
First published in Great Britain 1985 by
Julia MacRae Books
A division of Franklin Watts Ltd.
12a Golden Square, London, W1R 4BA
and Franklin Watts, Australia
1 Campbell Street, Artarmon, N.S.W. 2064

British Library Cataloguing in Publication Data
Smith, Joan
    We three kings from pepper street prime.—
    (Redwing Books)
    I. Title   I. Series
    823´.914[J]   PZ7
ISBN 0-86203-204-0

Phototypeset by
Ace Filmsetting Ltd, Frome, Somerset
Printed and bound in Great Britain by
Garden City Press, Letchworth

Contents

*For my god-daughter, Emma Ford,
who is nothing like Em, except . . .*

1 Our carol service

Pepper Street Primary is famous for its carol concert. We always have a full hall, because what goes wrong is always too good to miss, which is more than you can say of the singing.

Each Christmas, all through the Infants, I dreamed of the day I'd be in the Juniors, and take part in the carol concert. My name would be in the programme, I could see it. *Hark the Herald: Sam.*

Two years ago, the concert was great. Mr Tilly, who was in charge, was having a quick cig behind the stable, while the shepherds were nowelling, and he set fire to the crib. The straw was blazing up, but the Angel Gabriel put out the fire with lemonade meant for the party afterwards.

Last year was even better. Mr Tilly was in charge again. Pepper Street Primary went modern. The Virgin Mary did a rock song with her guitar, and the angels hand-jived and chewed gum, and the Wise Men were all punks, with green hair, ear-rings and studded belts. It was so impressive I almost cried. The vicar did cry. Mr Tilly never came back after Christmas.

And now it's nearly Christmas again; mince-pie time in cookery, greeting cards in painting, and in music, we're planning the new carol concert. It will be hard to make this year's as good as the last one, because Miss Bunny is in charge, and Miss Bunny is blessed with a dull mind. Miss Bunny doesn't like you to be happy. Also, Miss Bunny's mother should have made her wear a tooth brace early on.

"This year, we'll keep things simple," she says. "Concentrate on lovely voices."

"Which carols will our form be singing?" asks Malc. Malc spits when he talks.

"*While shepherds watched*, and *We three kings*," says Miss Bunny carefully, so as not to get us excited.

It comes to me with a flash. Forget the shepherds. I'm going to be a king. It's what I really want to do. Be a brightly coloured king, with jewels and cotton wool fur on my crown, not a shepherd with a duster on my head. I might be in with a chance here.

My sister, Em, is in the top form now, and the top form always do the Holy Family parts.

In her time she's been a back row angel, one of the children Herod killed, and a sheep. It was a mistake, as it turned out, to have people as sheep. There was too much bleating. We don't have sheep at all now. This year, Em's got her sights set on the Virgin Mary. That'll make Mum sit up; Em as the star part, and me as a king.

Miss Bunny decides to choose shepherds first. Even the girls are stretching their arms up, really keen to be shepherds. No-one will know they're only girls under their dusters. It seems everyone wants to be a shepherd except me. I slide down in my chair, so as not to be noticed too soon.

"Martin will be our first shepherd," says Miss Bunny. Good choice; he's used to animals. Sometimes he brings his ferret to school. Well, he did until it got free in assembly. We were praying for world peace at the time, which we didn't get, as the ferret bit the Head's ankle, and he swore out loud in the middle of the prayer.

Once Martin brought a pigeon, and it flew

12

round the room in nature study, bombing everyone. His father's just got a goat, which he's offered to bring along, too. Miss Bunny says on no account is he to do that. Martin will make a great shepherd.

So while Miss Bunny is dithering over who else to choose, I wonder what my first concert will be like. Lovely voices doesn't seem enough to me. I can't see lovely voices making the vicar cry. Mind you, he's feeble enough to cry at anything.

He runs the Pepper Street football team, which is quite different from the Sunday School team which he runs as well. He likes them; he doesn't like us. Wayne says he only does it

because he feels sorry for us. Well, we feel
sorry for him, so it's all square.

And I don't think he understands all the
rules, so it's really his fault that we never win.
It's certainly not ours. We practise all the time.
Every day we turn out, and Wayne, who is
captain, and I, plan the game in our minds. It's
getting the good ideas from our minds to our
feet that's tricky.

"I've got this good idea," I say to Wayne,
while Miss Bunny is still deciding about the
shepherds. "Came in a flash."

"What?" says Wayne. He opens his eyes.
The only time he breathes is when he's playing
football, or talking about it. He's a great
captain; he scored our goal. Wayne's all right.

14

"We're in this goal scoring position, see?
Instead of kicking direct, we pass across the
goal, and leave them looking the wrong way."

"A bit complicated, isn't it?" says Wayne.

"Well, what about . . ."

A dark shadow falls over me; it is Miss
Bunny's.

"I was speaking to you, Sam." She seems
rather upset.

"Sorry. I didn't hear." She'll never get the
parts sorted out if she doesn't get on with it.

"You can't even keep quiet while we plan the
concert, can you?" She puts her hands on her
hips, and sticks her nose in the air. "There goes
your chance to be a shepherd." Spiteful, she is.
Little does she know I didn't want to be a
shepherd, anyway.

"Don't worry Miss Bunny, really."

"Stand in the corridor for ten minutes."

I hang about in the passage, which is also our
cloakroom, hoping she won't have reached
giving out the kings until I get back. There's a
draught. I've read the noticeboard through
three times when I spy the Head coming round

15

the corner. I dive under the coats, disguising myself as a duffle and a pair of boots. It's the knees that give me away.

The Head pulls the duffle aside, and glares nastily at me. His nose is as thin as a darning needle; his mouth is a scrap of thread to go with it. I'd never call him a kindly man.

"To my office," he says. He thinks he ought to be firm, because it is the third time this week we've met in the corridor during lesson time. You'd think he'd have better things to do.

At last the Head and I are through with our little chat, and I get back to the class. I find everything is planned out.

"Who's what?" I ask Wayne, as Miss Bunny doesn't see fit to tell me. "Who's the kings, I mean?"

"Shiva is Balthasar."

Yes, I'd expected that. His mother keeps the tandoori take-away, but I reckon he's not far off being a prince. He never gets flustered when he doesn't know the answer.

"Go on," I say.

Wayne looks sheepish. "I'm Caspar."

I can't believe this. "You? Caspar?" Miss Bunny must be losing her marbles.

"What about Melchior?" I look at Wayne, wondering if he's saving a surprise for me.

He is saving a surprise for me. "Malc's Melchior," he says, looking down at the desk, and I get that same feeling as when the other side scores again.

2 Our team

I go home at dinner, because a jam butty is better than steak and kidney pie, shipwrecked on liquid cabbage, and I find not everything is lost. Em's done better than me.

"I'm going to be the Virgin Mary," she says, not able to keep from smiling.

I'm not surprised; she's got long fair hair, and she can sing in tune. Em's all right.

Already she's making plans. Right now she's stirring some evil blue liquid in a saucepan. "Got a long way to go before the concert's as good as last year," she says. "But I'm going to make HER something to remember." She stirs harder and splashes the blue liquid over the stove.

18

"What are you doing?"

"Dyeing my nightdress. SHE's always dressed in blue." There's not much to Em's nightdress; it's very suitable for summer when she wants to keep cool. "I'm not relying on Miss Bunny," she says.

Mum comes in, and blows her top. No, Em can't dye her nightdress, and fancy thinking she could, in the egg pan, too.

"I feel bad about not being a king," I admit to Em.

Em always knows exactly what to do with a problem. "*Anything* could happen," she says. "Learn all the words, and then you can step in at the last moment when one of them breaks a leg."

"But I wouldn't like any of them to break a leg."

"Get a cold then. Ringworm. Anything."

"What are you going to do about a dress?" I say, trying to help in return. "Though I expect the school one will be very nice."

"It won't, and you'll see what I'm going to do," says Em, and bounces out of the door. My sister is rarely defeated, certainly never by the likes of Miss Bunny.

So I take her advice, and start to learn some words while I practise dribbling a football round and round the front room settee. You have to keep it tight, or things get broken. Mum says I'm wearing out the carpet. So I put on my strip, to get in the right mood, and go out into the street, and practise shooting against the wall of Pepper's Pie Factory on the corner.

The vicar got us the strips, I can't think where from. The shirts have stripes going the wrong way, and they're made of funny material. Wayne says they were going to be leg warmers. They're purple, orange and lettuce colour, and you can almost see them in the dark. Not everyone likes them, but I do. Well, I like them, but at the same time, I know they're not right.

The vicar walks by, on his way to cast gloom on someone's doorstep.

"Practice makes perfect," he says, trying to smile.

20

"Got a match straight after school," I tell him.

"Oh, yes." The smile slips off his face, fast as money slips out of my dad's fingers. "We'll hope for the best," he says.

"Got a new plan. Wayne and me have worked it out."

"Splendid. Well, we'll hope for the best."

The match is against the Sunday School team.
Feeling we're in with a chance, we go out into
the park, under a dark sky, with quite a cocky
step. They all stare at us, especially at the
shirts. Their strip is shiny, and their shorts are
all the same shape.

We start off well. Wayne goes for a certain
goal, when he gets tripped up by this well-
washed full back. I look to the vicar, who,
through our dismal luck, is the referee. But he's
shaking his whistle, and squinting into the far
end of it. We explain about the foul, and the
vicar says, "It's only a game, and try to play

nicely."

Now this little cherub takes a kick at our goal, but he's clearly offside, so we let him go. The vicar has got his whistle on the road by now, and blows for a goal. We explain the offside rule, and the vicar gets sulky and tells us he's in charge.

Unfortunately, he now knows there *is* an offside rule, and he blows for it every time Wayne gets the ball. Only once more do we come near to scoring, when their pale-faced half clearly handles the ball. Where's the referee this time? Back there, leaning on our goal post, because he's got a stitch.

The Sunday School win ten nil; and a very dirty game they played, too. Still it stands to reason the referee would favour them. They all go off laughing and say they'll make it twenty nil next time. The vicar preaches a bit about being a good loser. Well, he should know.

To cheer ourselves up afterwards, we say that only twits go to Sunday School.

"They've got a crib," said Gareth, whose brother once went there, "with life-sized figures and animals, at the Sunday School." We think of our cereal packet crib on top of the lost property cupboard, and feel worse.

"I don't like big cribs," says Wayne.

"I don't like cribs made out of cereal packets," says Gareth.

To cheer myself up, I say, "Only twits are in the carol concert." This really upsets Wayne. He stumps off home without telling us off for losing. So we all walk back feeling bad. It's the Sunday School's fault.

When I get home, I find out where Em has been. To the Oxfam. The rich in our school shop at Marks and Sparks, but Em can outshine them all with what she picks up at the Oxfam. She got a Sam Brown belt, and a pair of striped braces. She's even got some long gloves like royalty wears for hand shaking.

But I'm a bit doubtful this time. For forty pence, she's got this electric blue dress, covered in sequins, with sleeves that show through to the pink skin of her arms.

"Will it be all right?" I ask. It's not what I

would imagine the Virgin Mary would care to be seen in.

Mind you, Em's got style. She's got flair, so she'll know what is all right.

"Look," she says. "People don't act Shakespeare the same all the time, do they? The whole idea of Shakespeare is to do it different each time. So why should Christmas always be the same? I'm doing it a new way. Pepper Street expects it."

"Miss Bunny won't expect it."

"By the time she finds out, it will be too late to stop me," says Em firmly. "How are your carol words coming along?"

"I've learned Melchior."

"Is that all?"

"I've learned it properly." It's no good expecting too much of me.

3 My part

It has to be my luck. It's the next day now, and
Shiva's got a sore throat. He speaks in a
whisper, and keeps clutching his neck. He goes
round trying to get people to look at his tonsils.
He can't sing a note.

"Anyone know the words?" asks Miss
Bunny. The label is sticking out of the back of
her jumper. She always looks more untidy
when things start going wrong.

"I know Melchior," I say helpfully.

"We don't need a Melchior, Sam, we need a
Balthasar."

"I know all the parts," says Malc. I can
believe that; I bet he knows the second verse of
the National Anthem as well. Anyway, it ends

up with Malc singing two kings, and me still not singing anything.

Then I have another blinding flash. So as to stay close to the rehearsals, and be on the spot when another king falls ill, I offer to help with the scenery. Mostly, it's the woodwork club who are making the stable. So I speak to Mr Beal.

"Can I help with the scenery, Mr Beal?"

"That's kind of you, Sam." Mr Beal's all right. In our school, any kind offer is quickly seized on; kind offers are as rare as a crisp spud finger from the Pepper Street chippy.

Now things are really hotting up. We're rehearsing after school, and making the scenery then, too. We go on until it gets quite dark outside. Through the windows, Pepper Street looks cold and dirty, although I think some of the dirt is on the glass. There is a wet chip paper, soggy and yellow, floating in the gutter,

and several blotchy milk bottles rolling about
on the pavement. Here inside though, the hall is
warm and bright, and very noisy as well.

I'm carrying a long plank, the last piece of
the stable roof, when Martin calls out to me
from the back of the hall. I swing round, and
my plank goes with me, all the way until the
back end bats Miss Bunny right across the
shoulder. She looks silly clutching her sleeve,
and pulling faces. She can't see the funny side,

29

of course. I hurry on over to the stable.

Wayne's not getting on too well with the part of Caspar. He can't say frankincense properly, and he's not at all regal. More like a nervous hamster than a king. He's never himself when he's away from a football.

"How do we think we should sound?" asks Miss Bunny. She takes that line when she's running out of ideas; our carol concert is a real test for a teacher.

Not slow to see the ball coming, so to speak, I put the plank down.

"I'll show you," I say, and elbow Wayne aside. Wayne doesn't even notice he's been shifted.

Feet apart, and arms crossed, definitely regal, I speed through the whole of Caspar's verse, well ahead of the piano.

"A lot better than Wayne," says Shiva. Shiva's all right.

This has an odd effect on Wayne. "I don't want to be a king," he says, all of a sudden. "I feel a twit."

"You make a lovely king," lies Miss Bunny.

She's prepared to overlook the fact he can't sing the words, because he stands still all the time. Miss Bunny likes people who stand still. She doesn't know his mind is on other things; either tactics, or flattening the Sunday School team.

"None of my friends is in it," says Wayne,

getting stubborn. "None of the team. They think the carol concert is for twits."

"Give it another try," she says, with what she thinks is a winning smile, but really makes

her look as if she's forgotten to sugar her tea.
She rubs her shoulder, as if it still hurts, which
I don't believe, and gives me a shifty glare. I
think she knows exactly what is going through
my mind.

"The blind has stuck," says Miss Brown.
Miss Brown is here to play the piano, while
Miss Bunny's getting people onto the stage in
the right order. When we have to sing all
together, Miss Brown plays with one hand only,
and waves the other hand about. Just now, she
is tugging feebly on the cord of the window
blind near the stage. I'm glad to see she wants to
shut out the grey picture of Pepper Street. The
blinds are a gift from the church, bought by the
proceeds of a sponsored run by the vicar. He
gave them so that we could have films shown in
the hall. So far, we've had *The life story of the
herring*, which was funny, and *How men lived in
the Stone Age*, which was not. I don't think
people would have given so freely if they had
known we wouldn't be getting proper films.

"I'll fix the blind," I say to Miss Brown. "It's
the little cog wheels of the roller which are the

trouble." It's funny how ideas come when you're out to please. I fetch the tall steps, and slosh some oil round the ends of the roller. I'm not mean with it. The blind pulls down quite easily.

"What a clever boy," says Miss Brown. Miss Brown's all right.

Two minutes later, the blind shoots up again, all by itself. Sounds like a rifle shot.

"This is a hold up," says Wayne. "Don't anyone move."

Miss Bunny moves. She walks over, and leans on the stable with her eyes closed. I hope she doesn't flatten it.

I pull the blind down again, but now it never stays put for long at a time.

I'm really enjoying being so helpful.

Next, I find the star which is to hang over the stable. We've used it every year, except last, and then we used a revolving coloured spotlight, because of being modern. The star is big and gleaming, and heavy. One of its points is squared off. Usually, we prop it up on the roof of the stable, but it doesn't look as if it belongs to the sky at all. I have this blinding flash.

I'm going to hang it on the light flex, and fix a piece of string to it. This piece of string will be threaded over the high heating pipe against the wall, which will act as a pulley. This way, we can make the star move across the stage for the kings to follow, make it sort of *yonder* along.

The high steps are tall enough, and I manage
to get up to the light behind a pyramid of
angels. I get the star knotted on, and let go of
it, to find out if it's going to twizzle round on
its string. With a crash, like an elephant hitting
the cymbals, the whole lot comes down, star,
flex, light and all. Everything goes dark, and I
can hear Miss Bunny getting over-excited.
She's shouting, "Get over here at once, Sam."

Well, I'm not getting off these steps in the dark, even to come to her aid.

It could have been a lot worse. It could have flattened the whole flock of herald angels. The star could even have flattened me.

As soon as the lights come on, she does a funny thing. Miss Bunny takes a piece of chalk, and makes a large cross on the floor of the stage. Then she grabs me down from where I'm wobbling about on top of the high steps, and hauls me across the floor by the scruff of my jumper.

"Stand there," she says, pointing to the chalk cross on the floor.

"Don't move. Don't move from that spot. You are going to be Caspar."

I hadn't realised my singing had been so impressive.

4 Em's part

Miss Bunny now holds my having a part in the carol concert against me. She knows I want that part more than anything else, even though Wayne says, "Who's the twit now?"

"Do one thing wrong," says Miss Bunny. "*One* visit to the corridor, and I shall give that part to someone else." She clamps together her mouth, snappy as a clothes peg, and I know she means it. I'm now forced to be a bigger creep than Malc.

Em is all the while putting temptation in my way.

"We've got to brighten this concert up a bit," she says, "if it's to be as good as usual." She's been to the Oxfam again, and for a further ten pence, has got a length of knotted red feathers. It looks like the neck of an embarrassed ostrich, but she calls it a boa. She flings it round her neck, and struts round the room. She looks less like my idea of the Virgin Mary than ever.

"I've tried speeding up the carols to get a bit of a beat into them, but Miss Brown can't keep up with me."

"It's meant to be lovely singing," I remind her, really growing into my part as a creep.

"By the way, I'm changing the words of my Coventry carol," says Em. "You could hardly say it's got a lot of zip. But the third verse is a lot better already."

She sings it to me.

"Herod the king is still raging,
At the dinner this day.
The powdered spud, the lumpy pud,
All children young will slay."

"You wouldn't dare sing that."

"I'll dare all right," says Em. "It'll go down a treat. And I've written this for you."

"I don't want new words."

But she insists, lowering her voice to a manly tone, and chanting:

"We three kings from Pepper Street Prime,
Are only here to have a good time,
And all the while, we'll make you smile,
But we're not so hot on rhyme.
You've got to say ho-ot."

Em will be famous for sure, but I always thought it would be as singer, or a model, not as a song writer.

"I can't let Miss Bunny hear that. I've got to

stay good."

"Save it for the night," says Em, "like I'm going to do."

"The words are really great," I tell her, "but I quite like the proper ones, too."

She looks at me, and her eyes light up. "You could do that dance with three legs," she says. "Like the man on the telly."

As it happens, we have a lot of carol gear at school. It had a rest last year, because of the concert being modern, so now it's twice as dusty as usual.

We make the main scenery new each year,

it's something to do in art lessons and the
woodwork club. But we always keep the
manger, and some shepherds' crooks. Also,
there's a case full of clothes, king gear and
Joseph gear, although the shepherds have to
bring their own dusters. Miss Bunny says that's
because of head hygiene.

The best piece in the case is the gold turban.
This has to be for Shiva, and he has a crimson
robe to go with it. I feel proud of Shiva. I hope
his mother closes the tandoori take-away for the
evening, so that she can be proud, too.

The crown, also, is quite good, silver foil
with cotton wool fur, and jewels. Malc gets

this, because he's been a creep for a whole term, not a few days like me. I've got to laugh. He gets a beard as well, which Miss Bunny seems to have made out of a dog moult. For sure, it's got living fleas.

This leaves me with a striped night gown, two sizes bigger than I am. I stand tall in case Miss Bunny thinks I'm not big enough to be Caspar any more.

"You look as if you're still in your tent," says Malc, spitting as usual. His gown is a royal blue bath towel, with a tinsel edge.

Come to the head gear, things get worse. Mine's a turban, too, but not like Shiva's turban; it's more like a stuffed tea-cosy. It would make a nice bed for the cat. Pavement coloured, it sits on my head like a huge mushroom, flopping over the thin white stalk, which happens to be my face. Even Miss Bunny smirks.

Em is pleased. She's going to wear a pale blue dressing gown. I know she plans to whip this off, as she gets on to the stage, to reveal her electric blue sequins. Unless Miss Bunny likes to get on the stage herself, and wrestle with Em, there's nothing she will be able to do about it. I'm feeling a bit worried over all this.

"What are you going to do about it?" asks

Em, when we get home again.

"Do about what?"

"Putting a bit of zip into this concert. We can't let Pepper Street down."

"I want to get it over with." I'm thinking about that turban, to say nothing of the tent.

"Well, I want them to clap me," says Em.

"They clap anyway. They like clapping."

"I want them to clap *me*," says Em. "Me, not the carol. I want to stand there, and hear them putting their hands together, all for *me*."

Em thirsts for glory.

No one is going to clap me, I know that, even after our carol. All the glory will be for Shiva, popular, handsome, and a true prince in his crimson and gold. At least the noise might drown the sniggers at the sight of me.

"You know, don't you," says Em, "that unless we do something, this is going to be the dullest, dreariest, most deadly carol concert ever?"

I agree with her. "The first failure," I say.

5 Too much practice

Even so, there is a feeling of excitement now
the day of the concert has arrived. There's a lot
of giggling, and no work done. We spend all
morning moving chairs into the hall, and Miss
Bunny has washed her hair. It's gone fluffy, like
a pram toy.

To show that he does not feel left out, Wayne
has called a football practice for straight after
school.

"It's light enough for pavement dribbling,"
he says.

"Twice round a couple of old ladies, and a
swerve past the lamp post," I agree.

"I want goal practice against Pepper Pies'
wall," he goes on.

"I've got to have my tea. I can't sing if I'm hungry."

"Look, Sam, twit, forget the carols. If you want to be in this team, you've got to practise. This team's going to be so good, they'll be selling our strip for action man."

It's sausages for tea, so I make mine into sandwiches, to eat outside. Mum is not pleased. I left the cabbage out.

The sky is grey, like it always is grey over Pepper Street. But this evening, it's heavier and uglier than usual; there's a bleak feel to the air, as if it knows the concert will be a flop.

"Right," says Wayne. "Aim straight for this brick, and he points to a blue one. "On the spot. Rat-tat-tat."

"England doesn't practise this hard," I tell him. The sausages have gone cold now, and taste greasy. I'm beginning to feel sick anyway, at the thought of what's to come. I know we'll never be any good.

"I want us to be proud of this strip," says Wayne. "These colours are our flag."

I pick at the clinging, knotted top, and the

colours dazzle my eyes, even in the half dark. How can anyone be proud of this?

Wayne kicks the ball hard against the wall, and the flakes of brick fly off.

"Right on target," he says.

I do the same.

"Great." Wayne grabs me by the arm. "Playing like this, we're in with a chance," he says. "You twits are going to be the best team this side of the town. If we believe in ourselves, we are in with a chance."

"I've got to go and get ready now," I tell him. "We have to be there an hour before to put on the make-up."

Wayne flings his palm against his forehead. "Make-up?" he yells. "How can I make a team out of painted kings? Carol concerts are for Sunday School twits, not for footballers."

"You only got one king," I point out. But I wait for a bit because I don't like to see Wayne upset.

"Twenty shots. I want twenty goals," says Wayne. Then, after that, he makes us stand to attention, and say, "*We* are the best. We *are* the best. We are the *best*.''

So I'm late back to school, with no time to change first. I put my anorak over the strip, knowing for certain my striped tent will cover totally, whatever I'm wearing.

6 In with a chance

It's the make-up which takes the time. Odd.
Miss Bunny knows how to use greasepaint. I
think it's the only thing she does know. Instead
of the usual black eyebrows, and pollyanna
doll cheeks, we look like real people, but not
like ourselves.

"Ooooh," says Em, impressed with her new
face. "Aaaah." Miss Bunny scrapes back Em's
hair, and she doesn't look a bit like my sister.
She looks deeply good.

Miss Bunny does a cover up job on me. I end
up mostly as whiskers. She moves on to Shiva,
to sprinkle a bit of gold glitter on his cheek
bones.

There is a very odd smell about, which turns

out to come from Martin's goat. He's brought it along to be a sheep. That goat's got an evil eye. Mind you, it can't be all bad. It's eaten Miss Bunny's gloves.

Miss Brown puts two buckets of water behind the door onto the stage. She doesn't say anything, but I know she's remembered when Mr Tilly set fire to the crib.

Peeping through the stage curtains, I can see the hall certainly is full. The whole of Pepper Street football team except me, of course, are in the back row. Already they look restless. I think they might make trouble.

In the middle, at the front, sits the Head. He looks as worried as I feel. His fingers are

clenched tight. The vicar, on the other hand, looks happier than usual. He's taking very deep breaths. Perhaps he's training for the next time he's referee.

Now the concert is starting. Em gets on the stage early. I look towards the corner where she's been dressing, and I can see she's forgotten her boa. She'll be sorry about that. The herald angels are letting rip. One is crying. Another has caught her foot in the hem of her dress, and can only hop.

Soon, it's Em's turn to sing. I remember the new words. What is Miss Bunny going to say?

But Em changes her mind, and sings the proper words. They're not a bit zippy, but they sound just right. It won't be that she's chickened out; it's because she'll be feeling good, with her new face. She gets an ordinary sort of clap. That won't please her.

The shepherds stampede their way on to the stage. Martin's got hold of the goat. For some reason it's got tinsel wound round its horns.

"Get that animal out of here," shrieks Miss Bunny, forgetting she can be heard at the front.

"I'll get it on the stage," says Martin, and makes a dash for it.

I can tell the shepherds are making a mess of it out there, all pushing to get to the front, and looking in different directions at the star.

"Ouch!"

I bet that's someone the goat has bitten.

It's the same as everything we do. A mess.
Pepper Street Primary makes a mess of
everything. I wish I'd never thought of being a
king. To take my mind off the whole sorry
business, I think about the team. That's a mess,
too.

It comes to me in a flash. Why the team is a
mess, what we've been doing wrong, why we
never reach the goal. We try to pass the defence
the same way every time. They know what to
do with us. But I've seen proper players on the
telly give the ball a little trickle backwards, and
that really works. No one I know can do that
when they're tackled. All we've got to do is
learn this little trick. I've got to try it straight
away.

There's no football. There's nothing at all
like a football lying around. The only kickable
thing in the room is my turban.

I'll try it with that. Right. Bring the toe
across the top of the ball, sorry, turban, flick it

back, and . . . splosh. It's flicked itself straight into one of the buckets of water.

"Us next," says Shiva, coming over to me. All evening he's been leaning calmly against the wall.

I grab my hat, and try to wring it out. The stuffing's all gone lumpy, and it won't give up the water. It's like a sponge.

I put it on, and look in the mirror. It hangs down all round my face, like runny icing droops over the sides of a cake. Besides that, the water's trickling down my neck. There's hardly any water left in the bucket.

"Come on," says Malc. "We're on now."

He's spitting a lot with nerves.

"I can't go on like this. They'll laugh at me."

"We can't have only two kings," says Malc, not caring about me at all. "We'll look silly then. You'll have to come on without your hat."

Shiva says calmly, "We'll go ahead and search for the star, then you can join us when we've found it. You'll have time to get that thing wrung out."

I try again. It gets lumpier than ever. Perhaps it's dry clean only. But nothing is going to revive this turban; that much is quite clear.

Luckily Miss Bunny is keeping a close eye on the shepherds while all this is happening. She's pulling faces at them to stop them shuffling about. The last thing I want is Miss Bunny getting into a state about my turban.

Panic is making my mind active. The idea comes in a flash. I must make use of what is to hand.

Miss Brown's gone three times through the

introduction music by the time I get on the stage. There's Em sitting in the stable, still with the blue dressing gown on, a single sequin winking at her neck. She looks sad, but truly good.

Holding up my robe to avoid tripping over it, I stride briskly up to Malc and Shiva, ready to catch the music next time round.

And there comes this mighty burst of clapping from the back of the hall, even before I've opened my mouth.

It's the team. They get to their feet. They give me a standing ovation. Other people join in, in case I'm someone famous under the whiskers, and I expect they don't want to look

ignorant. Wayne is clapping as if there's no tomorrow.

Now it comes to me.

They're not cheering me at all. The team are clapping their strip; they're applauding my turban.

The strip has made a splendid turban, purple, orange and lettuce leaf, the colour blazing under the lights, strapped on with Em's red feathery boa. The team is saluting its flag, so to speak.

Shiva smiles proudly at me. Malc looks furious. Em looks quite sick with envy. They haven't realised what it's all about. I certainly shan't tell them.

The vicar is sitting with his head in his hands. I wonder what he's praying for now.

I'm never going to forget this moment, well, not until I leave the Primary anyway. With Em looking so pure, and Shiva like a true prince, and the shepherds smelling farmlike because of the goat, and the back half of the hall all

clapping me. I think this concert beats them all.
I think it is our best ever.

I sing my part really loud, and everyone joins
in the chorus.

But it gets even better. The window blind
shoots up, the one I'd mended, sounding like
the crack of a rifle.

Outside, I can see the snow coming down.

Flakes of wandering, feathery snow coming
from out of that heavy sky, as we should have
guessed it might, and Pepper Street is white.
White roofs, unspoiled pavements sparkling
under the street light, even white gutters, clean
white gutters. Pepper Street looks pure, like
I've never seen it look before.

It comes to me in a flash. Even we, even Pepper Street Primary, can't spoil Christmas.

Miss Brown is winding up her arm for the next carol. I can never make out when we're supposed to start.

"See amid the winter snow
Born for us on earth below."

Our voices sound clear, we mean every word we sing now. Even Wayne is swaying to the music, at the back of the hall. I look round at us all, at the Virgin Mary, at the crib, the herald angels, and the shepherds, standing still at last. Even the goat has lost its mean look. And now I know that the crib is not only for the Sunday School; it's for us too.

Something has washed *us* clean. Something has put *us* in with a chance.